Christopher Sarna

from
Na Na Sarna

The Christmas Wreath

Written by **James Hoffman**
Illustrated by **Jack Stockman**

First American Edition, 1993

10 9 8 7 6 5 4 3 2 1

Copyright © 1993

School Zone® Publishing Company

ISBN 0-88743-575-0

Library of Congress Catalog Card Number 93-084726

The elves' work was done for the year and they were tired. They were too tired to put up their own tree on Christmas Eve.

They knew Santa would be disappointed when he returned, but they had barely finished the last sleighload of toys.

"How about... a wreath?" yawned Chief Elf.
The truck-making elf just snored.
The dollmaker tucked a doll pillow under
her head and sighed.

The other elves blinked and shrugged.
The last few nights they had even made
toys in their dreams!

Chief Elf gathered his last bit of energy to make a wreath from scraps of workshop materials, pine boughs, a berry or two and a leftover candy cane.

Even the wreath looked tired.

As he hung the wreath on the workshop door, Chief Elf said to himself, "Oh well. It's the thought that counts."

Late that night a hungry polar bear smelled the pine boughs and peppermint and thought of food. She followed the scent to the door where the wreath hung.

As the polar bear rose up on her hind legs to take the candy cane, she bumped the wreath, which fell off its hook and slipped over her head.

A very surprised polar bear now wore a wreath necklace!

She tried to get it off, but the more she wiggled and shook, the tighter it became.

Perhaps, she thought, it would come off in her world of ice and water.

She lumbered across the ice and dove to the bottom of the bay through golden kelp and glistening seaweed.

Still the wreath did not come off. Instead, it collected strands of seaweed and sea flowers, and a small silver fish got tangled in the bough!

Each time she came out of the water to breathe, the arctic air froze the water on the wreath. Layers of ice were added, trapping underwater sea life in each layer.

Soon the polar bear grew tired.
She climbed slowly onto the frozen,
icy shore to rest.

In the moonlight, shafts of green and blue and silver and gold reflected off the wreath. The polar bear would have been proud of her necklace if she knew how beautiful it now was.

But she had to get it off. It was so *heavy*. She tried to snag it on jagged rocks and then tried to get it off on a fence post in the Reindeer Yard. Nothing worked.

In desperation she went back to the workshop door and stretched up, scratching the wreath against the door.

Remarkably, the hook that Chief Elf had used caught the ice on the wreath, and the polar bear was free.

She fled happily, rid of her icy necklace at last.

Up above, Santa and his sleigh and reindeer were nearing home. Below, he saw dazzling rays of colors that shone like beacons to guide his way.

As Santa and the reindeer drew closer to the workshop, they stared in wonder at what they saw.

On the workshop door hung a wreath wrapped in ice crystals, shimmering and glittering in the moonlight.

The familiar jingle of reindeer bells woke the elves. They were still half asleep as they stumbled out to greet Santa. They, too, were amazed to see the wondrous creation on their workshop door.

The elves looked at each other in surprise when Santa thanked *them* for the beautiful wreath.

They'd created a jewel-like Christmas wreath? An ice sculpture? How and when had they done that?

The Chief Elf stroked his beard. How had his tired wreath become so glorious, he wondered? *He* remembered putting out a scraggly, little... well, *mess*.

He smiled as he gazed at the icy beauty, wondering about miracles and Christmas Eve.